Mountains, Meadows and Moonbeams

Books by Mary Summer Rain:

Nonfiction:

Spirit Song
Phoenix Rising
Dreamwalker
Phantoms Afoot
Earthway
Daybreak
Soul Sounds
Whispered Wisdom (Fall, 1992)

Children's:

Mountains, Meadows and Moonbeams

Mountains, Meadows and Moonbeams

A Child's Spiritual Reader

Written and Illustrated by
Mary Summer Rain

HAMPTON ROADS
PUBLISHING COMPANY, INC.

Hampton Roads Publishing Company, Inc.
891 Norfolk Square
Norfolk, VA 23502

Or call: 804-459-2453
    FAX 804-455-8907

If this book is unavailable from your local bookseller, it may be obtained directly from the publisher. Call toll-free 1-800-766-8009.

ISBN 1-878901-39-7

10 9 8 7 6 5 4 3 2 1

Printed in the United States of America

This very special book belongs to a

very special person by the name of:

_____

Dedicated to all the beautiful children of
the world, that they may be encouraged to
nurture and cherish the sacred heritage of
their shining Spirits

A Note To The Parents And Guardians

Benjamin Franklin saw what he called electricity and believed in it while others who could not see it scoffed and ridiculed him. Where would we be today if all the great inventors of Yesteryear had been shamed into denying their beautiful discoveries because of the fear of being labeled strange or different?

You, as parents and guardians, have fostered the belief in many a Santa, Toothfairy and Easter Bunny, therefore, do not question your child's belief in other things he/she may see and hear. The time has come to open up your minds as the little children and to take joy in the new discoveries you find there.

Remember, the real truth in the saying: "Seeing is Believing" is "Believing is SEEING."

Truly, the most precious and valuable commodity of any Nation is that Nation's children. For the children of today are the hope and salvation of the future of the planet Earth. Their imaginative abilities in conjunction with their vast creativity can, indeed, bring our world into new and enlightened heights that we have yet to envision. The children of today will be the new spiritual pioneers of the New Age of Peace and Harmony. It is our spiritual responsibility to ensure that each child's understanding of the truths is as comprehensive as possible.

Part One

The Spiritual Basics
Of The Universal Truths

Part One Contents

The Real You

God is a beautiful and shimmering White Light filled with warmth, understanding and great love.

One day God became very lonely and wanted some company, so He sent out many, many shining sparks from His beautiful Light. These sparkling pieces of God are called Spirits.

The Spirits are pieces of God and they are good. They love God very much.

When the Spirits started to come to the Earth, they lived in a human body God called "Man." One God-Spirit lives in one human body. Your God-Spirit lives forever, it can't ever die.

Your body is like a house that your God-Spirit lives in. You should be proud to know how much God loves you and to know that the "real you" is that beautiful spark of God's Spirit living inside you.

You must love all people because God is in every one of them. God's shining Spirit is in each person you see around you.

When You Became A Baby

One day, before you were even born and you were still a beautiful, sparkling Spirit, you thought that you would like to live on a planet. You looked around at all the planets and decided you wanted to live on the Earth. Then you looked real close at all the people living on the earth and you picked out a very special person. This special person was the one you wanted to be your mother.

When you decided who your mother would be, you were very excited to be with her, but you had to wait until your new mother was ready to have her baby. That baby would turn out to be YOU!

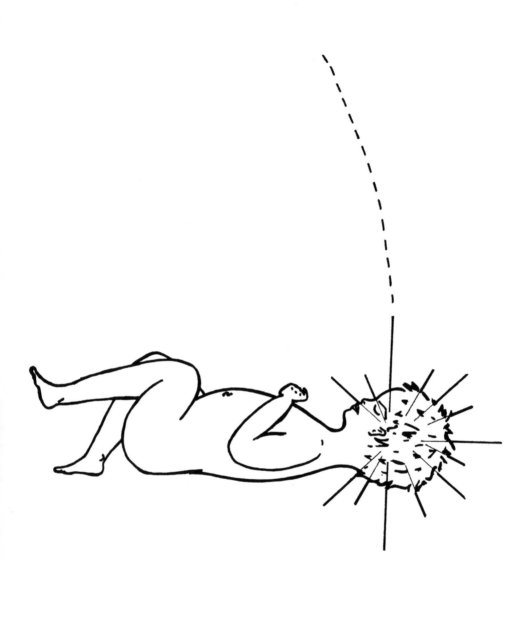

While you were waiting for the time when your new mother would have her baby, you spent a lot of happy time watching over her and being near her. She did not know you were around because you were still all beautiful Spirit, but she loved the baby growing in her very much. You loved her too.

When your mother went to the hospital, your shining Spirit floated over her and, as soon as the newborn baby was born, you gently lowered your Spirit down into the tiny baby. It was at that exact minute that the baby - YOU - took your very first breath.

Now you had a human body to live in and you could touch and love your mother.

Thank you God for letting us pick out our parents.

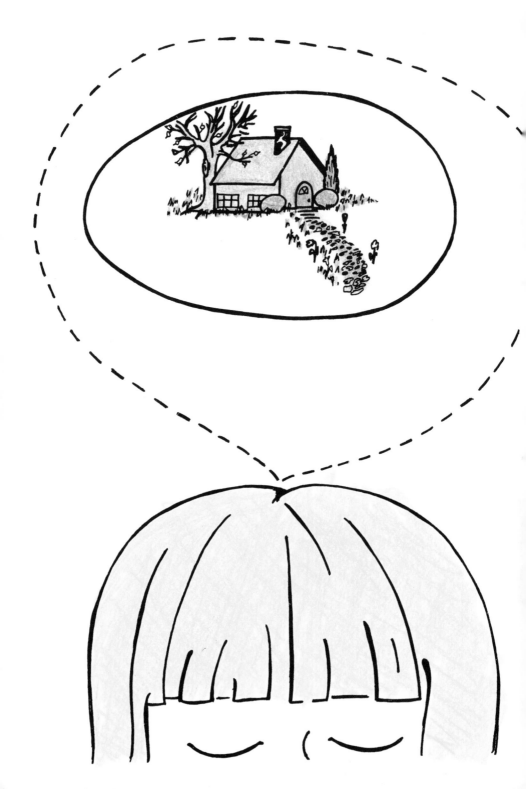

Your Circle Of Protection

You have a very exciting and very amazing way of keeping yourself safe from harm. God gave your mind a tool called the White Light of Protection. This is very white and very bright.

In your mind, you can imagine this White Light in the shape of a big, big circle, and you can put things inside it that you want to protect - even yourself.

When a bad thunderstorm comes, you can imagine your house safe inside this Circle of Protection and you can see in your mind how, even your yard, is all lit up with the White Light.

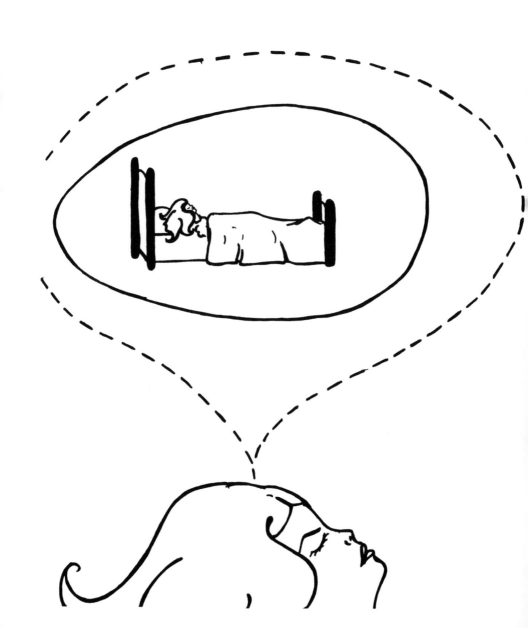

Sometimes, when you are out at night or when you are especially scared of something, you can put yourself in the White Light of Protection Circle and you can see in your mind that all around you is the bright and glowing White Light, and you know you are safe.

Your White Light of Protection Circle protects you when you go to sleep too. You use your mind's protection whenever you want to keep anyone you love safe from harm.

The Things You See

When people think, their thoughts become real things and can move around through the air. Most of the time we cannot see these thoughts moving around us and we don't even realize that they're there.

Sometimes when you are very quiet, you may see someone's thought. Maybe it will be pretty, or maybe it will be scary. If it makes you scared, just put yourself into your White Light of Protection Circle and it will go away.

You must always remember never to think bad things about anyone because your bad thoughts can hurt people. Think only good things about others.

The thoughts people have can become real things. When this happens, these thoughts are called "Thought Forms." Thought Forms can float around in the air. Many people see these Thought Forms out of the corner of their eyes, but they see them for only a second and do not think about them again.

You also may sometimes see Thought Forms. You may also see Spirits without their human bodies. You know they cannot hurt you though because you have your White Light of Protection Circle to use. You don't have to be afraid of Spirits you may sometimes see because, when you were still a God-Spirit, you could see people too.

You must like living here on Earth and try to be very good because that is why your Spirit wanted to live inside a newborn baby. You wanted to be here to live a life that would make God proud of you.

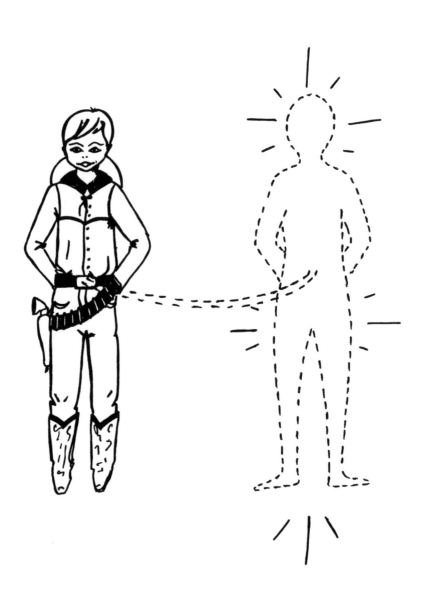

Your Shining Body
And Safety Line

You are so lucky. You have TWO bodies. One body you use when you are awake. It is called the *Physical Body*. The other body is called the *Spirit Body* and it is bright and shining.

Your two bodies are always held together by a glowing *Silver Cord* at the middle of your waist. The *Silver Cord* can never, ever break or tear, and it can stretch farther than the stars in the heavens.

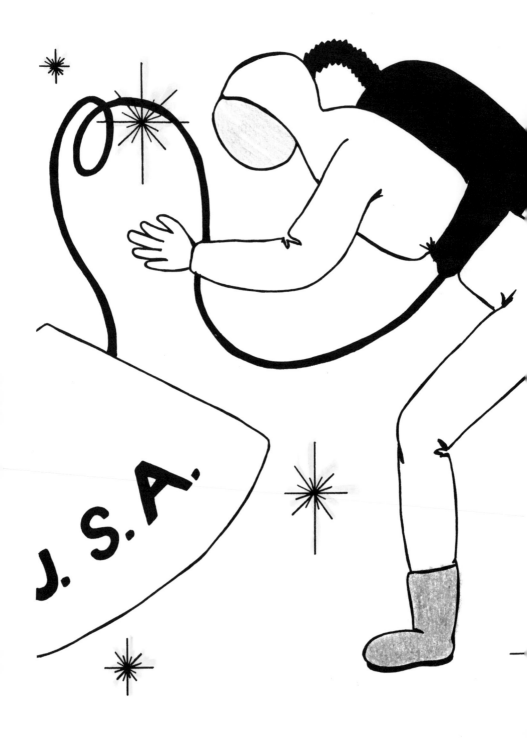

When you are asleep, your Spirit Body likes to gently float out of your Physical Body. Your Spirit Body goes to special places while you're sleeping. Sometimes it wants to go and be near God. Sometimes it wants to learn more about God and, sometimes it even helps others while you're asleep.

Later, when you're older, you will be able to send your Spirit Body out of your Physical Body if you want to. You do this during very quiet times when you are resting.

You're like an astronaut in space when you send out your Spirit Body on its Silver Cord. When you wake up, the Spirit Body quickly comes back into you all safe and sound.

You are very lucky God gave you two very special kinds of bodies.

Dreamland — Real Land

Everyone dreams every night. Dreams are very wonderful things. Dreams can solve many of your problems if you ask them to. Dreams can show us the past and even the future too.

Your Spirit goes to many wonderful places while you sleep. Your Spirit does many different things when you are resting. Sometimes dreams can tell you what your Spirit did while you were asleep.

Scary dreams are only dreams that show the things you are afraid of. You know you never should be afraid of scary dreams because they can never hurt you. You need to talk about your dreams with one of your parents. Sometimes talking about them with another person helps you to see that they were not so scary after all. Talking about your dreams can be very helpful.

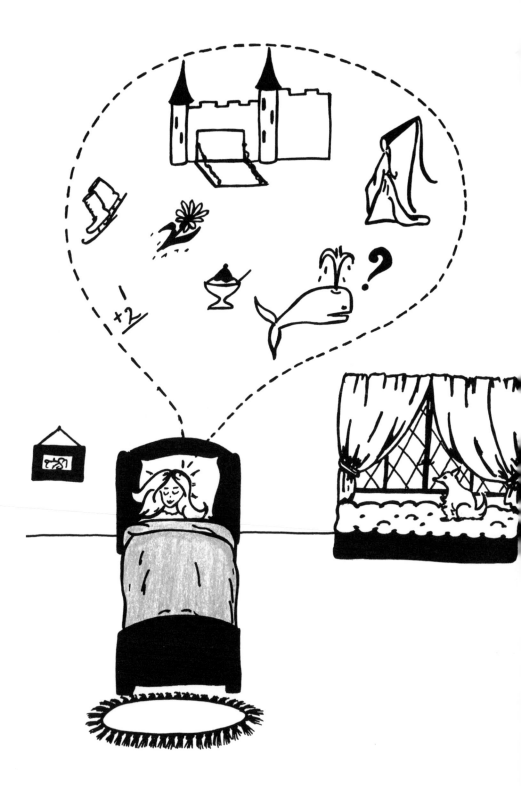

Sometimes your dreams are all jumbled up and they don't make much sense, but that is only because you can't remember all of them.

In dreams we can go to the Akashic Records where we can see things that have happened long ago.

Many times we just dream things that we think a lot about. In some dreams we can talk to God and hear God talk to us.

You should look forward to going to bed at night because dreams can be so much fun.

Whisper Softly

God loves us all very much. He gave everyone a very important helper called a "Guide."

Your special Guide has a Spirit Body just like you had before you were born. This Spirit Body is just like the Spirit Body you have now. The same one that travels out while you're sleeping.

Your special Guide may have been a special Spirit friend you had before you were born. Or maybe your special Guide is a relative who is now a Spirit. Because your Guide is all Spirit, he can go everywhere with you. Your Guide watches over you when you're playing and even when you're in school. Sometimes when you're asleep at night, your own Spirit Body will travel out on its Silver Cord to be with your Spirit Guide. Sometimes you go places together and then dream about them.

Sometimes your Spirit Guide will whisper to you in your mind. Usually you can hear him if you are in some danger and he is warning you to be very careful.

Some people can even see their Spirit Guides. Your Guide loves you very much and wants you to be good so that someday your own Spirit can live with God again.

Thank you God for giving us a Spirit Guide to watch over us.

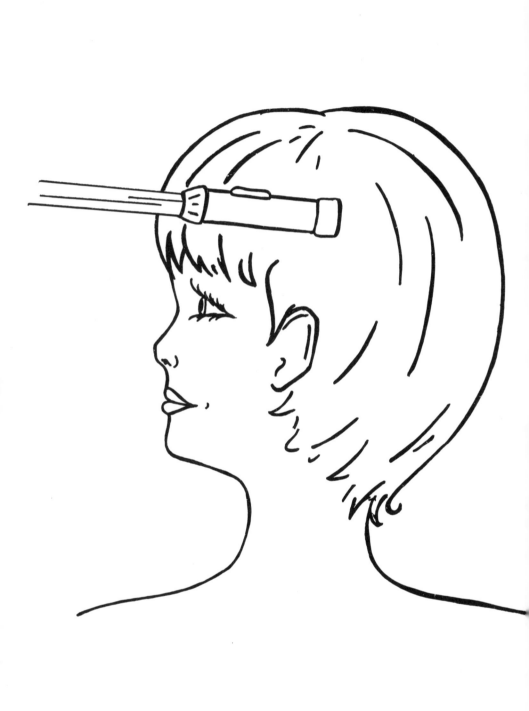

The White Light Beam
Of Protection

You have a very powerful light. It's something very much like a flashlight in your head. Nobody else can see it because you use it from your mind. It is filled with the White Light of Protection and it never runs out of Light. It always works because it can't break. You always have it with you.

Sometimes, when you are all alone or in a scary place, you don't ever have to be afraid because when you aim your White Light Beam of Protection around, it makes you safe and sound.

From your mind, right in the center of your forehead, your White Light Beam can shoot a light into the dark. It can shoot a beam of light into the scary monsters of your mind and make them go "poof."

You can't see this beam with your eyes, but you can imagine it. Your Beam can't ever hurt anyone because you can only use it on the things you think about that frighten you.

The White Light Beam of Protection is a very special tool God gave your mind to help whenever you are afraid. As you grow and learn more, this Beam will be very useful in your life.

Quiet Time — Discovery Time

You can talk to God whenever you want. When you pray you talk to God. Sometimes you can hear God talk to you in your dreams, but you can only feel God TOUCH you when you meditate.

You close your eyes and sit or lay very still. You image yourself inside your White Light of Protection Circle. Then you close your eyes and imagine a big white movie screen in your mind. When all your thoughts have gone by the screen, it becomes white again.

Now your mind's eye can begin to see many new and wonderful things on the screen. Many of these things on the screen will come from your own Spirit and some will come from your Guide.

During meditation, you may hear beautiful music. You may feel full of a wonderful and warm love. You may feel the softness of a cloud on your face. You may be able to sit on a star and see the whole world. And you may see colors you never saw before.

During meditation you may discover so many, many wonderful things, but best of all, for just an instant, you may even be with God.

That is what meditation is.

Your Living Diary

In a special place, out among the stars where there are all the Spirits and Guides and God, is a very big book called the "Akashic Record."

In this Record Book is written all things that ever happened and even all about the future, too. It has all the words you have ever said. And because your thoughts are real things, the Book even has all your thoughts in it too.

When some people are sleeping or are very quiet, or are meditating, they can send their Spirit Body out to read the Akashic Record and bring back very important information.

God knows everything and keeps a daily record of all you do. You must always think good things and be kind to everyone, for everything you do is written down in the Akashic Record. It is just like a diary of your life.

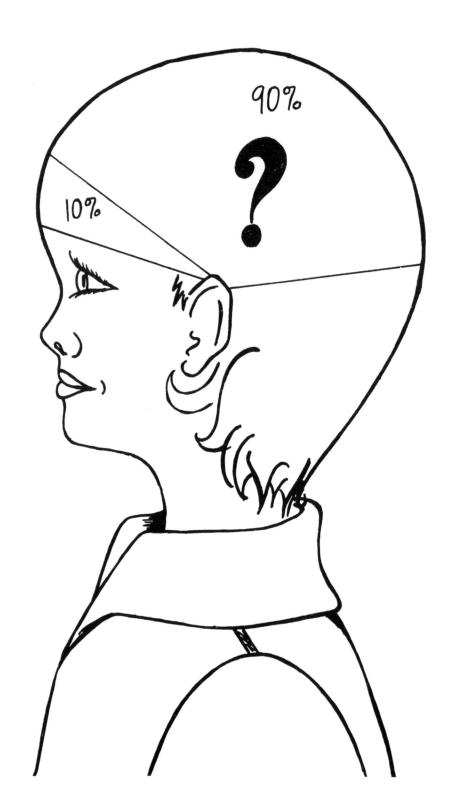

What Is Parapsychology

"Para" means "beyond" and "psychology" means "study of how our minds work." When the two words are put together they make the word Parapsychology which then means: the study of how our minds work beyond the every-day thinking we do.

Scientists and researchers have told us that we only use 10% of our brains. That is only a very tiny part. What does the other 90% of our brains do then?

These same scientists and researchers are now learning much more about that other 90% of our brains. They have made a whole new field of study about it and they have called it Parapsychology.

Scientists had to make many different studies of Para-psychology because they have found so many different things that the other 90% of our brains can do.

Some of these very special things our minds can do are Telepathy, Psychokinesis, Clairaudience, Premonition and Precognition.

All of our brains can do these different things. Some people can do one thing better than others. People who can use this other 90% of their minds real good are often called a "Psychic." "Psychic" means "mind."

Since ALL people can use this other 90% of their mind a little bit, ALL people are psychic. Most people don't even realize that they're using this part of their mind. These mind powers were given to us by God and are called "Spiritual Talents or Gifts."

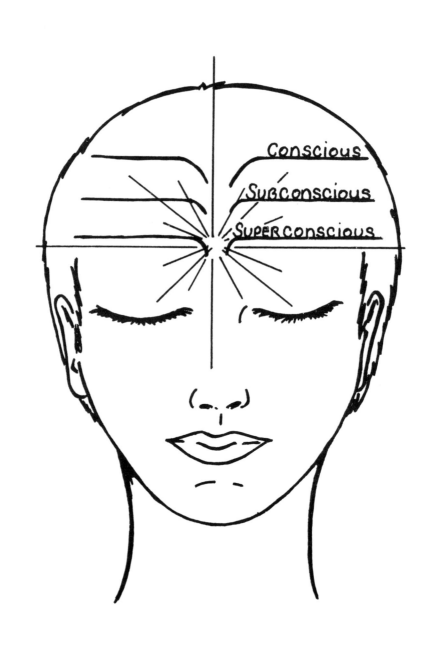

Universal Consciousness Of God

Our minds are made up of three different levels of thinking. The first level is our *conscious* mind which we think with all day long. The second level is our *subconscious* mind which stores up all of our memories. And the third level of our mind is our super conscious which is so powerful, we don't know much about it yet. The Superconscious level is where the Spiritual Gifts or Psychic Talents come from.

The Superconscious level of all our minds began from what is called the Universal Consciousness of God.

There is a great Stream of Thoughts flowing through Time and it is made up of Spirit matter. This mass of flowing thoughts is called the Universal Consciousness of God.

In our mind, between all three levels of thinking, is a Path, or Connection. When we can move our thoughts and vibrations in perfect line on this Path, we can then be in touch with the Universal Consciousness of God.

The Universal Consciousness of God has recorded all history, all thoughts, and all events since before Time began. It contains all the events of the future and it has great, great wisdom. If we are of pure Spirit and if we quiet our mind, we can sometimes mentally travel along the Path to the Universal Consciousness and learn many amazing and beautiful things.

Many famous psychics receive their information by connecting their super consciousness with the Universal Consciousness.

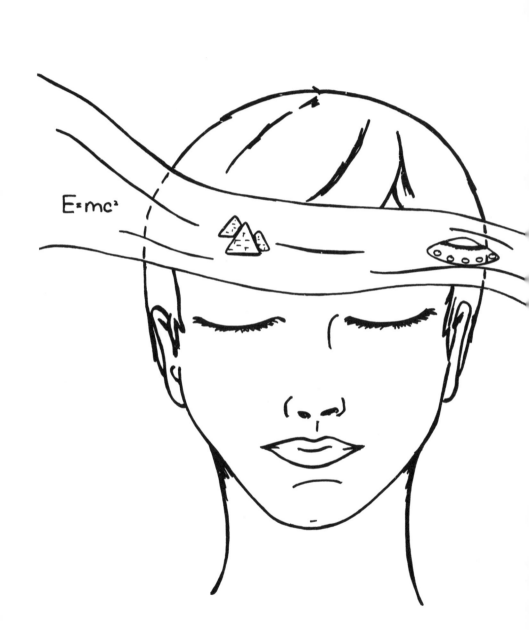

Precognition And Retrocognition

"Pre" means "before" and "cognition" means "know." When we put the two words together, they make the word Precognition. Precognition would then mean "knowing before."

When we say that someone has precognition, it means that their mind can know things that are going to happen before they actually do happen. In other words, they know the future.

"Retro" means "back" and "cognition" means "know." When we put the two words together, they make the word Retrocognition. Retrocognition would then mean "knowing the past."

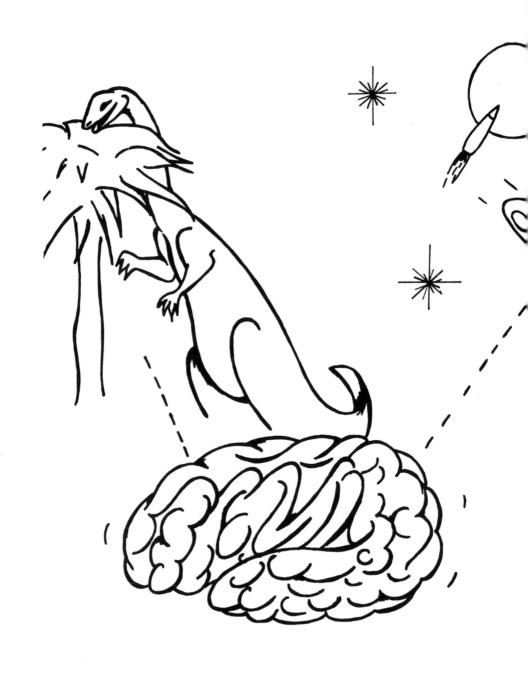

All things that have ever happened and all things that ever will happen, including the things that are going on right now, are all recorded in the Universal Consciousness.

Whenever our mind connects with this Universal Consciousness and we see things from the *future*, we have an experience of *precognition*.

Whenever our mind connects with the Universal Consciousness and we see things from the *past*, we have an experience of *retrocognition*.

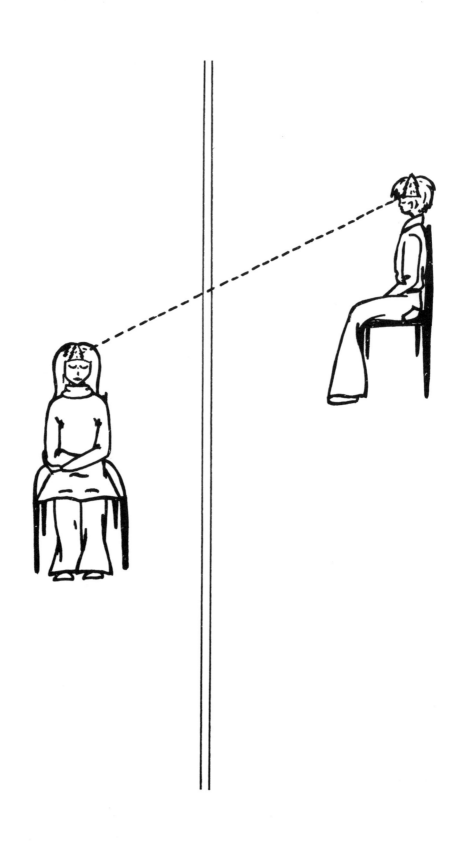

Telepathy

"Tele" means "distance" and "pathy" means "feelings." When we put the two words together, they then make the word *Telepathy*, which would then mean *feelings we get from a distance*.

We have learned that all thoughts are real and that they have energy. Our mind is like a radio that sends out the thoughts through the air. These thoughts travel through the air at different levels. The different levels of air that our thought energy travels on are called *vibrations*.

If someone is sending out a thought on the same level of vibration that our mind is thinking, we can then know their thought.

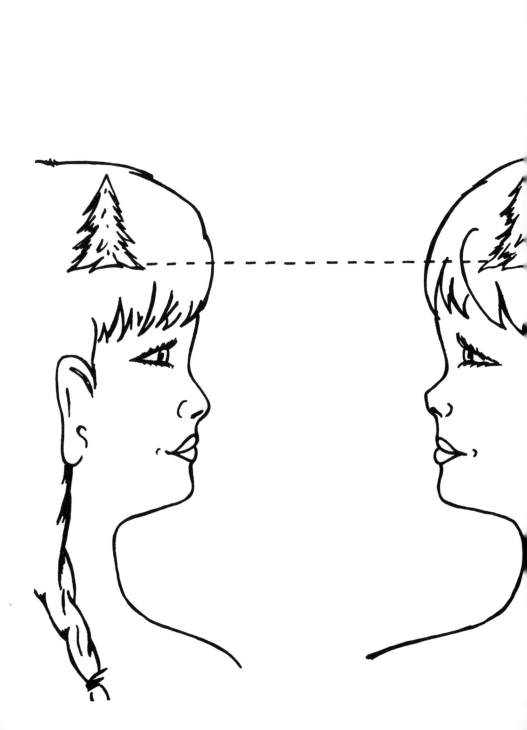

Scientists have tested peoples ability to know the thoughts of others. Scientists have tested peoples Telepathy. They put a person in a room and have them think of something special, like a tree. Then they put another person in a different room, sometimes they are put in a different building or city even. If the person in the different room can know the other person's thought of a tree, then that means both people were thinking at the same level of vibration.

If you ever know what somebody is thinking, then you have Telepathy. It is said that you have *Telepathic Abilities*. This is a Spiritual Gift of God. All Spiritual Gifts must be used to help others.

Vibrations

The energies that move around and out from your body are called vibrations. All people have vibrations coming out from their bodies. We can't always see these vibrations, but many times we can feel them.

The vibrations always match the person's mood and personality. If a person is calm and happy, their vibrations will be coming out slow and smooth. We feel very good when we are around these people.

If a person is very nervous or angry, their vibrations coming out from them will be fast and uneven. We feel very uneasy, uncomfortable and nervous when we're around these people.

All living things have energy that sends out vibrations into the air. Animals are very good at sensing your vibrations. A horse can tell if you're afraid to ride it by sensing the frightened and nervous vibrations you're sending out.

Many people are very good at sensing the vibrations of others. You're doing it all the time. You choose your best friends and get along so well with them because you sense that their vibrations are almost the same as your own.

Our feelings about a person are telling us what he is like by sensing the vibrations he is sending out.

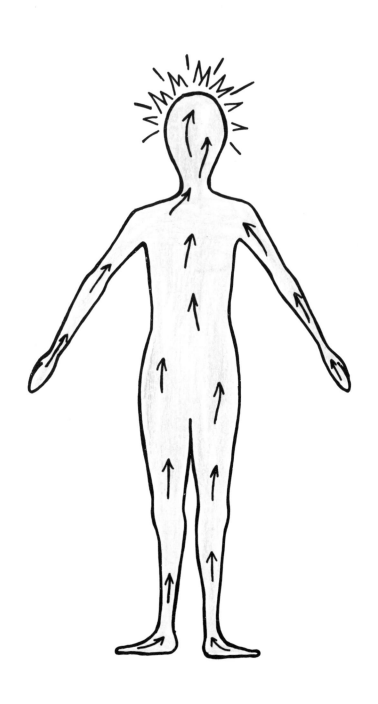

Psychokinesis

"Psyco" means "mind" and "kinesis" means "move." When we put the two words together, they then make the word *Psychokinesis*, which means *moving things with the mind*.

The mind holds a very large amount of energy. This energy is very strong. If we think real hard and tell our mind's energy to move something, it can move.

Our whole body is filled with great amounts of energy. When we try to gather all of the energy of our body into our mind, we can make our mind very strong.

Scientists in Russia have some people who can move the pointer on a compass and the hands of a watch with their mind energies. These people are said to have *Psychokinetic* abilities.

A FUN EXPERIMENT

Blow up a balloon and string it from a ceiling light fixture or a hook. Be sure all the windows and doors are closed so that no breeze or air movement can move the balloon. Sit real still and stare at the balloon. Think real hard about moving the balloon. Think real hard about all the energies in your whole body going up into your mind. All the energies are collecting at the center of your forehead. When you feel that your mind is real strong and full of energy - send all that energy out at the center of the balloon. Imagine all that energy shooting out like water from a squirt gun. Did it move? Just a tiny bit? The more you practice, the more you will be able to move it a little.

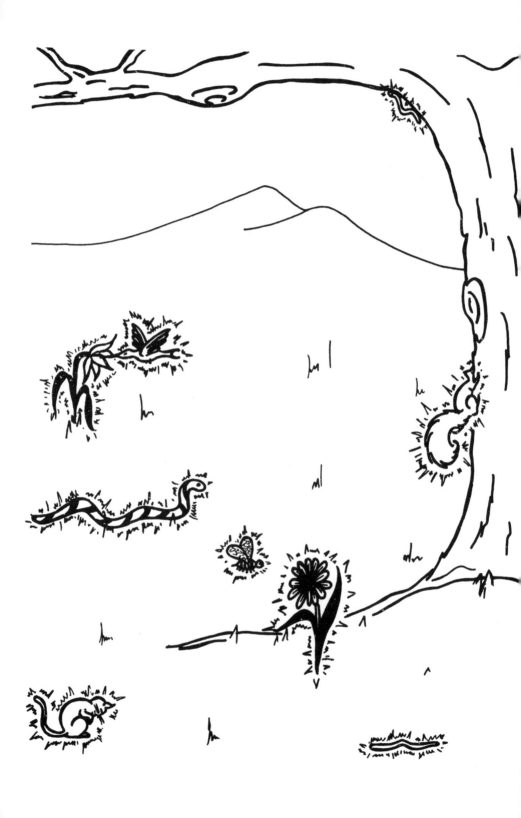

Auras

All living things including our physical bodies are filled with energy. This energy is like electricity and it radiates out from our bodies. These energy radiations are called *Auras*.

Some people can see the Auras of others. These Auras are very colorful and are like shimmering lights. They are always moving and can tell many things about us.

Auras tell us two main things. One is how healthy our bodies and minds are, and the other is how spiritually developed we are.

Most people can see Auras but don't realize it. When we say, "Gee, that green shirt looks so good on you," we are sensing how good the color green in the shirt matches the color green in the person's Aura.

A very amazing camera has been invented by a Russian man by the name of Semyon Kirlian. This camera can take pictures of the Auras around all living things. The pictures from this special camera are called *Kirlian Photography*.

Clairvoyance And Clairaudience

"Clair" means "clear" and "voyance" means "to see." When we put the two words together, they then make the word *Clairvoyance*, which would then mean *to see clearly*.

When our mind unites with the Universal Consciousness and we see things that are happening *now* — in the present — we are said to have a *Clairvoyant experience*. People who have these are called *Clairvoyants*.

Many of us have had some feelings of danger or perhaps have had the feeling of good news of a friend or relative that is far away. We can't see them, but we "know" what they are doing when they are doing it. This is knowing something *Clairvoyantly* and it is a Spiritual Gift from God.

"Clair" means "clear" and "audient" means "to hear." When we put the two words together, they make the word *Clairaudient*, which would then mean *to hear clearly*.

When our minds unite with the Universal Consciousness and we hear things that are happening *now* — in the present — we are said to have a *Clairaudient experience*. People who have these are said to be *Clairaudients*.

Many of us have heard things in our minds that others around us did not hear. It may be the quiet whisper of our Guide or it may be some beautiful music. It is very normal to hear like this and when we do, we are said to hear *Clairaudiently*. This is a Spiritual Gift from God.

Healing

We have learned that all of our thoughts are real things. Our thoughts have much great energy and they can be very, very strong. There is a very White Light that our mind can use to help heal our bodies when we are sick or hurt.

The White Light is very bright and it glows. We use this White Light by imagining it in our mind. When we send the energy of our mind together with the White Light to the sick part of our body, we can help it very much. We can use this to help heal ourselves.

People who can use their mind energy with the White Light are called Psychic or Spiritual Healers.

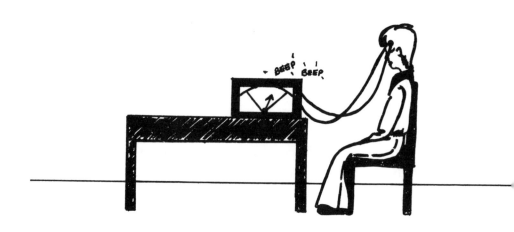

Scientists are now finding out about this special power of our mind to heal. They have invented a machine to help teach the mind to control pain in the body. This machine is called a Bio-feedback machine.

EXPERIMENT EXERCISE

The next time you have a headache, sit down where it is quiet and be very still. Close your eyes and relax your body. Think real hard about the pain in your head. Imagine a brilliant, shining White Light on the pain and say to yourself: Pain, Pain, Pain. Do not tell the pain to go away, just let the pain know you are aware of it. Send all your thought energy into the center of the pain. If you have done this right, you will be surprised to find the headache is almost completely gone. Practise this and each time it will be easier.

NOTE: Going into the very center of pain is like traveling into the very center or eye of a hurricane. The center is always quiet and calm.

Out-Of-Body Experiences
Or Oobe's

We all have a physical body that we use everyday. We also all have another body called the Spirit Body that we can learn to use whenever we wish to.

The Spirit Body is invisible. It is connected to our physical body by the Silver Cord, remember? And that Silver Cord can never break.

Many times, when we are resting or being very quiet, our Spirit Body will separate from our physical body. Our mind always travels with the Spirit Body so that we can think of where we want to go and remember where we went when our Spirit Body comes back into the physical body.

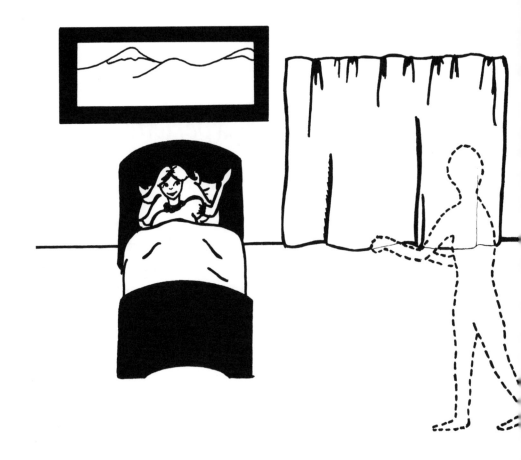

Many times, when we are asleep, our Spirit Body will lift out from our physical body and travel around to many wonderful places while our physical body sleeps. When we wake up we don't always realize that we were really at those wonderful places because we think they were just dreams.

Sometimes we can see other people's Spirit Bodies. Maybe your Aunt thought about you before she went to bed and her Spirit Body traveled to your room while she was asleep. If you were calm and sensitive, you either saw her in your dream or you were awake and saw her real Spirit Body in your room. I hope you said, "Hi!"

Colors

Colors have vibrations. Colors can affect our moods. We have colors in our Auras that tell how we are feeling inside -- whether we are happy or sad.

Our body's Aura can have many different colors. It also has a main color that is brighter than the rest. When the color of our clothes we wear blend or match the main color of our Aura, then we usually feel very good about what we are wearing.

When the color of our clothes clash with the main color of our Aura then we don't quite feel right about what we're wearing and we usually end up changing our clothes.

What is your favorite color? Your favorite color most always is the main color of your Aura too.

What Colors Mean

<u>**RED**</u> means that you have a lot of energy. It can also mean that you get angry very easily.

<u>**PINK**</u> shows that you are shy.

<u>**YELLOW**</u> means that you are usually healthy, happy and friendly.

<u>**GREEN**</u> means that you have a strong ability to heal. It means that you like helping others. Most doctors and nurses have much bright green in their auras.

<u>**BLUE**</u> means that you are very kind and are a good person. This means that you're thoughtful and caring.

<u>**PURPLE**</u> means that you try to live a life close to God's laws.

<u>**GRAY**</u> shows that your physical body is not well or that you are not thinking right.

<u>**BROWN**</u> means that you are down-to-earth. It also can mean that you don't always think positive.

<u>**WHITE**</u> is the very best color of all. It means that you have a pure heart and spirit.

Part Two

Spiritual Lessons From Animals

Part Two Contents

The Caterpillar's Secret

You think I'm lowly probably,
 'Cause I crawl upon a tree.
Just for awhile, will I crawl around the ground,
For soon you'll see my secret, which surely will astound.
I'm a creepy, crawly caterpillar,
And my secret is a thriller.

Right now I'm not so pretty,
But for me please have no pity.
It's not what you see on the outside,
What counts is the Spirit *inside*.
I'm a creepy, crawly caterpillar,
And my secret is a thriller.

I'm not so nice to look at,
I'm really quite sure of that.
I am rather ugly in fact,
Until I perform my act.
I'm a creepy, crawly caterpillar,
And my secret is a thriller.

Even 'tho I'm plain,
Much beauty I contain.
My heart is full of love,
So of me, often think of.
I'm a creepy, crawly caterpillar,
And my secret is a thriller.

Quiet! Be still! My secret now you'll see,
For my momentary absence, I send apology...
Look UP! UP in the AIR! For, what you now behold,
Is the beauty of my Spirit all gracefully unfold.
You see how lovely is my prime,
Best of all...'twas there all the time!

90

Lesson

What the caterpillar tells us is very important to all people. You see, even though he was very ugly to look at — very ugly on the outside, he proved that he was most beautiful on the *inside*.

Every person on earth has a wonderful, shining Spirit that is a part of God's Spirit. It glows and sparkles like the brightest star in the heavens.

Never, ever judge a person by how pretty they are. Never dislike a person because you think he is ugly. God made ALL people. He wants us to love ALL people.

Some very beautiful people may be very mean. Some less beautiful people may be very kind and loving. Remember the caterpillar's words: "It's not what you see on the OUTSIDE, what counts is the Spirit INSIDE!"

The Pee Wee Kiwi

I'm a night bird called a Kiwi,
Of the flock I'm the pee wee.
They treat me like a baby,
So I'll prove to them, just maybe.
Even 'tho my body's small,
My mind is quite sensational!

I always sit and listen,
While my mind begins to glisten.
My eyes are always very sharp,
To find our food out in the dark.
Even 'tho my body's small,
My mind is quite sensational!

My ears are now very keen,
I warn of enemies unseen.
I've saved the flock from harm,
By sounding my alarm.
Even 'tho my body's small,
My mind is quite sensational!

They see it's NOT how big you are,
To have a mind spectacular.
It's really the SPIRIT in you,
That must come shining through.
Yes, even 'tho my body's small,
My SPIRIT's quite sensational!!

Lesson

What the little kiwi is telling you is that just because your body is not as big as an adults, it doesn't mean that your mind can't do great things.

Your mind is where all your most powerful Spirit abilities are. They are there just waiting for you to use them. You use them when you know what another person is thinking. You use them when you see or hear things that others do not. You use them when you meditate. You use them when you pray.

When your mind and Spirit work together there is nothing your mind can't accomplish. So remember, even though you're a child, your Spirit has great power to do great things.

What The New Kangaroo Knew

I'm a new baby Kangaroo, I'm called a Joey,
And my little heart is all warm and glowy.
I'm safe and dry through a hard rainy storm,
And through long cold nights, I'm comfy and warm.
Wherever I am, my mother is with me,
Just knowing this fills my Spirit with glee.

I nap and doze in the soft furry couch,
When I'm nestled down deep in my mama's pouch.
From dawn to dusk I can stay all curled,
Without a thought or care in the world.
Wherever I am, my mother is with me,
Just knowing this fills my Spirit with glee.

I'm never afraid when a danger lurks,
Because of the way mom's protection works.
For all my needs, I'm well provided,
And in all my ways, I know I'm guided.
Wherever I am, my mother is with me,
Just knowing this fills my Spirit with glee.

Even 'tho just a babe am I,
I talk to my mom by and by.
I thank her for comforts and loving me,
Because of her love, I'll always be free.
Wherever I am, my mother is with me,
Just knowing this fills my Spirit with glee.

Lesson

The little kangaroo is a wise babe. He knows he is being cared for and looked after.

Each person, both big and small, is also being cared for and looked after too. Who does all this caring? Why, God does! God loves you very much. Because of His great love for you, He protects you, He guides you through your life and He provides you with a home and food.

You must not worry about things because everything that happens, happens for a very good reason -- God's reason. Put all of your faith and trust in God and how He does things. As long as you have your trust in God, you can be free of worries in life.

Take time out from your play sometimes to talk to God. Tell Him how much you appreciate all He does for you. Tell Him thanks. Tell Him you love Him. Know What? You'll make God feel real good inside.

Just as that little kangaroo is nestled all comfy and safe in his mama's pouch, so are YOU nestled comfy and safe in God's hands. Always.

Abigail Snail

Of all the critters God has made,
I'm the very slowest I'm afraid.
But don't you worry - there's a reason,
And for me it's most pleasin'.
I'm Abigail Snail and my pace is slow,
All of my days I go on tiptoe.

All day long others race past me,
They run like that rabbit late for tea.
I don't know why they hurry so,
You'd think they'd be tired all a go.
I'm Abigail Snail and my pace is slow,
All of my days I go on tiptoe.

I see the others all a scurry,
They scramble and ramble in such a flurry.
They flutter and scamper head-over-heels,
I'd like to know just what's the big deal?
I'm Abigail Snail and my pace is slow,
All of my days I go on tiptoe.

In the end, it's not so wise,
Someday these racers will realize.
For they stumble, tumble, fall and sprawl,
Flat on their faces after all.
I'm Abigail Snail and my pace is slow,
All of my days I go on tiptoe.

Until they learn to slow their way,
I'm oh so happy all the day.
For my slowness I'm most prayerful,
'Cause it makes me be so careful.
I'm Abigail Snail and my pace is slow,
All of my days I go on tiptoe.

Lesson

What happens when you hurry? Abigail Snail knows, do you? When you're in a rush, you usually are not very careful. You usually drop things or can't think clearly.

It's very important to always be most aware of what you're doing, where you're going and how you're going. Especially HOW you're going. Fast? Carelessly? Why? If you're already late for school, it really doesn't matter if you're a few minutes later.

When you hurry, your mind doesn't keep up with your actions, which causes you to be careless. If you hurry across the street and your mind can't have the time to remind you to look both ways first, it didn't do any good to do all that rushing if you get hit by a car.

Remember to always keep your mind most aware on whatever you're doing. In order to do this you must not ever be in such a big hurry.

NEVER LEAVE YOUR MIND BEHIND.

The Knoll Mole

God made my body very wee,
But that does not hinder me,
You see, my eyes are almost blind,
But my mind sees things most Divine.
For in my mind lays the key,
To open doors, let my Spirit free.

I live in a green, grassy knoll,
For my house, I burrowed a hole.
It doesn't matter that I live underground,
For the secret of sight I have found.
For in my mind lays the key,
To open doors, let my Spirit free.

Animal friends feel sorry for me,
They come to visit me under my tree.
If only they saw the things I see,
Such things to share, all of we.
For in my mind lays the key,
To open doors, let my Spirit free.

I'm happy in my hole-in-the-knoll,
I really have everything under control.
So there's no reason to console,
For my soul has reached its goal.
For in my mind lays the key,
To open doors, let my Spirit free.

Lesson

God gave our bodies many organs to do many different things. Ears to hear, eyes to see, a tongue to taste with, a nose to sniff and nerves all over to feel with. God also put all those organs together into one special organ located in our mind. This special part of our mind is where all the special Spirit powers and abilities come from.

Long, long ago, people used this mind organ very good. They could feel, hear, smell, see and taste, just by THINKING of a texture, sound, scent, picture or food. But then they became lazy and stopped thinking so much. They used their bodies more than their minds. The mind organ then became lazy too. Soon they found it harder and harder to use it.

God gave us this mind ability and He meant for us to use it. We can begin to make it work again through meditation and practice.

The little mole didn't care that the eyes on his face were almost blind because he knew God gave him an eye in his mind and ... he USED it!

The Skunk With Spunk

They tell you not to play with me,
And if you do, you'll be so sorry.
They say I have some awful stinks,
And that I'm really quite a jinx.
The talk about me does offend,
I just want to be your friend!

You have not even met me,
So how can you agree?
If you would come and meet me,
I'm sure that you would see.
The talk about me does offend,
I just want to be your friend!

They say I have a real bad smell,
And that often I repel.
But no one even knows me well,
So tell me how they tell?
The talk about me does offend,
I just want to be your friend!

If to the gossip you do listen,
A fine friend you'll be missin'.
If you would use your OWN mind,
A new playmate you will find.
For talk about me does offend,
I just want to be your friend!

Lesson

Have you ever listened to someone talk bad about another? If you did, let me ask you...why? What good came out of it? Any? Of course not. When you listen to gossip, you are really showing others that you cannot think for yourself or choose your own friends. It is a very, very bad thing to talk about others in an unkind way.

If people know you don't want to hear gossip, it makes them feel a little ashamed for spreading stories about others. Perhaps they'll stop doing it.

You are a beautiful part of God's Spirit just as everyone else is. No matter WHAT bad thing a person has done, they shouldn't be talked about. Walk away from a gossiper. Use the fine mind God gave you to make your own judgments of people.

Everyone in this entire world has done at least one thing that they are sorry for. Because we ARE a part of God, we must forgive them and leave all the true judging to God alone. You wouldn't want people to gossip about you, so walk away from those who gossip about others.

Why The Giraffe Laughs

I play on the sunny terrains,
Over Africa's wide, grassy plains.
With friends I romp and play,
And in the shade we lay.
I'm a giraffe that's happy inside,
For the aid that I can provide.

A very long neck have I,
It reaches to the sky.
I do not offer excuses,
It has very special uses.
I'm a giraffe that's happy inside,
For the aid that I can provide.

To you I will convey,
God planned it all this way.
I'm in such a happy mood,
'Cuz I help in getting food.
I'm a giraffe that's happy inside,
For the aid that I can provide.

When food is hard to get,
My head up high I set.
I pass the food to those below,
On them my aid I will bestow.
I'm a giraffe that's happy inside,
For the aid that I can provide.

Lesson

Each person has a special reason for being born. Each person also has special abilities that God gave them. Some people are real good at math, some are good at reading, while others can spell real good.

God also gave each and every one of us Spirit Gifts. These are abilities of the mind. Maybe you can sense vibrations real good or see auras to tell if someone is becoming sick. Maybe you have the ability to tell others what their dreams mean.

God doesn't want us to keep these Spirit abilities to ourselves. He doesn't want us to be selfish with them or hide them. God wants us to share them with people so we can help others be closer to God.

Whenever we can, we must always try to help others. Just as the tall giraffe became so happy by reaching high up to get food for the shorter animals, so should we always help others whenever we can. See how happy you will become inside when you share your Spirit abilities with others.

The Wise Bunny

If in a bunny hole you creep,
You will not hear a peep.
No, we are not all asleep,
There's a secret that we keep.
When less and less is said,
You learn more in your head!

Even when we're underground,
We do not make a sound.
For ideas in our mind abound,
When silence is around.
When less and less is said,
You learn more in your head!

Chatter and patter, sputter and gab,
Really it can be quite drab.
If you're always in a scream,
Your mind will never beam.
When less and less is said,
You learn more in your head!

If you'd just keep your mouth still,
I know you'd get a thrill.
To listen and to find,
Such treasures in your mind.
When less and less is said,
You learn more in your head!

Lesson

Have you ever known anyone who talked and talked all the time? Have you ever known anyone who hardly said anything? Which one do you think was smarter? Some people can talk for hours and hours and, when they're done talking, they really haven't said much at all. And some very quiet people are very deep thinkers and would rather listen and learn.

The bunny never, ever makes a sound. He is always listening. . .thinking. . .learning.

We can learn a very good lesson from those silent little bunnies. Just remember what they believe — **WHEN LESS AND LESS IS SAID, YOU LEARN MORE IN YOUR HEAD!**

The Peacock From Little Rock

Look everyone! Look to see,
Look at all the elegance of me!
The feathers I wear, aren't they fine?
See how they quiver, glisten and shine!
I really do not understand,
Why you don't think I am grand.

Oh yes, I can see your pain,
Unlike me, you are so plain.
Please do not feel in despair,
Just because I have such flair.
I really do not understand,
Why you don't think I am grand.

I'll talk to you even 'tho you're drab,
Perhaps about ME we can gab!
Why aren't you more reactive,
To my colors most attractive?
I really do not understand,
Why you don't think I am grand.

My dressings are just beautiful,
Which really makes me wonderful.
My feathers are so plentiful,
I must be irresistible!
I really do not understand,
Why you don't think I am grand.

Lesson

Look around you and see what people wear. Are you attracted to people who wear fine and beautiful clothes? Why? Are you attracted to only those schoolmates who wear the 'in' styles? Why?

God made each and every person all the same. He made them all equal to one another. Each person has a beautiful, sparkling Spirit within him. This Spirit is a part of God. This Spirit is what we should see in every person instead of what clothing they are wearing.

Mr. Peacock was very proud of himself because he looked so fine on the outside, but was he kind? No! Clothes are worn to keep us warm, they don't show what our Spirit is like or they don't show what kind of person we are.

Never concern yourself with what someone wears. It is really so very unimportant and you are wasting your energies and time being concerned over such things. Spend your valuable time and energies by loving each person for what they **ARE — NOT** for what they wear.

The Funky Monkey

You must think I'm clever,
I could copy you forever.
In all you say and in all you do,
I can do all things, just like you.
Me too! Me too!
I do, I do.

Don't you think I'm smart,
That I have such an art?
Some think I'm just a chump,
'Cuz I thump an' bump an' jump.
Me too! Me too!
I do, I do.

Back and forth on vines I swing,
Yes, I can do most anything.
To you I know that I must seem,
To copy people most supreme.
Me too! Me too!
I do, I do.

I bet you thought you'd never see,
A monkey sitting having tea.
As you are sipping on your brew,
Isn't it nice, just me an' you!
Me too! Me too!
I do, I do.

Lesson

The monkey is a very funny animal to watch. If you pat your head, so will he. If you clap your hands, he will too. The monkey always copies whatever he sees people doing. It's okay to copy everyone . . . IF you're a monkey!

Each and every person is different. Nobody has your name. Nobody has your face. Nobody has your mind. When you have to copy others and do what they do or say, you lose yourself in them. You are no longer the beautiful and unique individual that means YOU!

Be proud of who you are. Be proud to think for yourself. Be proud to be different sometimes. Be proud to be able to use your OWN mind. Leave the copying to the monkeys where it belongs.

BE YOU!

The Tale Of The Ant

Some people say I'm tiny,
But I will not be whiney.
Some people say I'm very small,
Really I'm quite exceptional!

If you only knew me,
I'm sure you would agree,
That I am really very strong,
And about me you were wrong.

Even though I am so wee,
I have a great big family.
When you see us in your yard,
We're really working very hard.

Just because I'm little,
I shouldn't be belittled.
Even though I live in the dirt,
My feelings are very easily hurt.

In God's plan I play my part,
And very tender is my heart.
Next time you're on a walking spree,
Please think to step OVER me!

Lesson

The little ant is one of God's smallest creatures of nature. Even though the ant is so tiny, it still has a very important part to play in the whole way that nature works together. God doesn't want us hurting any of his animals or little creatures. They all have energy and are a part of the whole living and breathing life of our planet Earth.

We should stop to think about that little ant that we're about to step on. It has energy. It has a reason for living. It is busy at doing a job for its own community. It has life.

We must love all forms of life. Just because something is smaller than we are does not mean that it is not important. It doesn't mean that we can just kill it because it won't matter. It **DOES** matter!

Please always remember to love the life in all God's little creatures. If you can do this, you will grow up to be a kind and peaceful adult who will respect and love all people too.

Part Three

Spiritual Messages From Verse

Part Three Contents

Mother Nature's Message

Dear little children, please gather 'round.
Bring you a pillow and come and sit down.
Listen well Dears, be quiet and still.
Give all your attention please if you will.

I once gave people a beautiful Earth,
To be enjoyed, cherished and loved from their birth.
Majestic mountains that reached to the sky,
With lush and green valleys for the butterfly.

I gave them air that was fresh, clean and clear,
And it dizzied the head of each mountaineer.
I gave them clear oceans, lakes, seas and streams,
And in them reflections would glisten and gleam.

I gave people soil so rich, pure and fertile,
I gave it with love to show my goodwill.
I gave them the seed of love and of peace,
With hopes that these feelings would greatly increase.

But little children, I'm counting on you,
To refresh the Earth as the mountain dew.
I'm counting on you to end the pollution,
And lovingly work to find the solution.

Message

Mother Nature has been so wonderfully good to us by providing us with everything we need to live in comfort. She has given us good soil to grow all our food in. She has given us fresh rain to water that food and to clean our bodies and to quench our thirst. She has given us golden sunshine to warm us and to coax the sprouting seedlings from her soil. She has given us snow-covered mountainslopes for our sporting enjoyment, just as she gave us the glistening lakes for our pleasures too.

I'm sure she is very saddened at all the oil from ships she sees in her seas. She feels awfully bad about the chemicals that people put into her sweet soil and it hurts her to see her clear air so terribly polluted. Mother Nature is counting on you, the children who will one day be grown-ups, to make her Earth as beautiful and pure as it once was in the beginning.

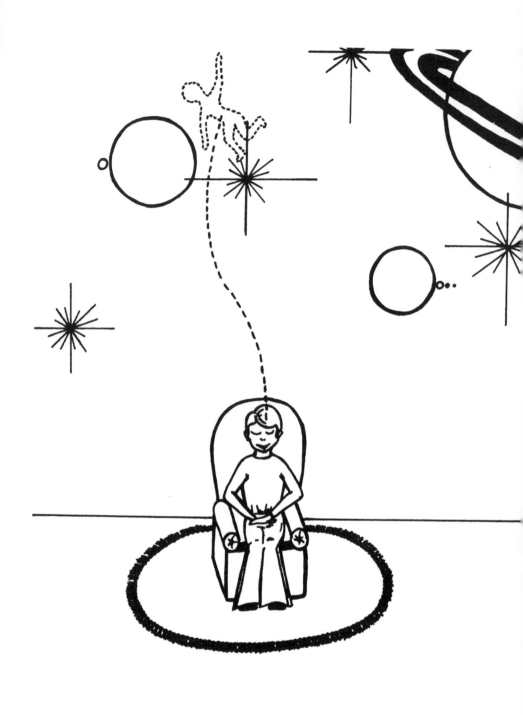

The Universe In Me

When I sit quiet and my mind is still,
I softly meditate and Oh what a thrill,
To unfold and spread the wings of my Spirit,
And soar to the heights of the Infinite.

Jupiter, Mars, Pluto and Saturn,
Are only small specks of the beautiful pattern.
Milky Ways, Stars, Planets and Moonbeams,
Are all included in the wonderful scheme.

Soaring, flying, reaching and winging,
From light to light in Celestial glimmering.
From no beginning and to no end,
The boundless Cosmos has proved a Godsend.

With plan of Will and Wings of Spirit,
I can be in places most exquisite.
Places in reality and places in fantasy,
Go wherever I want in the galaxy.

But the place I love best,
And the reason to be blest,
Is when, for an instant so grand,
I reach out and touch God's hand.

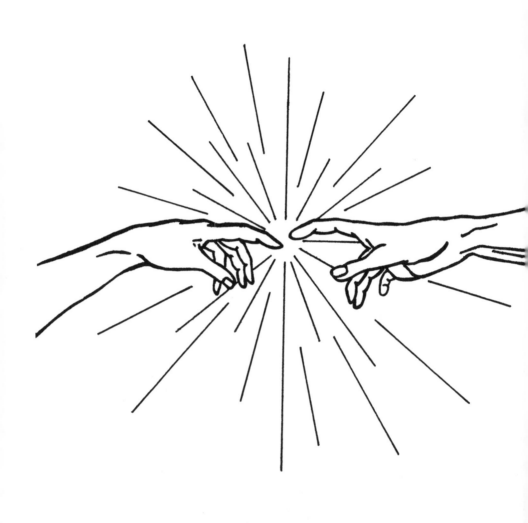

Message

Meditation is a Spirit Way given by God. It is God's Pathway for our Spirit to rise above all heights, both physical and non-physical. It is our Spirit's heritage to be able to soar to the farthest reaches of our Universe and to discover the billions of galaxies far beyond our own.

In meditation we find that our bodies and Spirits are but one tiny cell in the living, breathing whole of Nature and in All That Is. God wishes to keep in touch with us at all times so He gave us the Way of Meditation for us to reach our final goal.

When our Spirits are willing and when our hearts are pure, we can open the door of love and reach out and touch the all-embracing Spirit of God which is waiting there for us.

The Spirit Of The Mountains

The mountains live and breathe and love,
There dwells the Spirit from above.
The signs are there for us to see,
And together create a symphony.

Sit in a glen and be ever still,
And let the discoveries give your Spirit a thrill.
Sounds, sights and feelings are there all anew,
To delight and amaze that never you knew.

Pines, Aspens and Lodgepoles too,
Murmur to the wind in rendezvous.
Bubbling brooks and dancing streams,
Laugh and giggle in each moonbeam.

Then, when the sounds that you know disappear,
You are aware of a change in the atmosphere.
Fear not, little one, for what you now hear,
Is the Great Mountain Spirit whispering near.

Fairy, Elf, Gnome and Pixie,
All join in God's tapestry.
These loving Spirits are all part of one,
Now the Mountain Spirit's tale has been spun. 144

Message

Being among Nature is the closest we can bodily be to God. More varieties of nature exist in the mountains than anywhere else on Earth. God loves all His animals and even the plants and the trees have a special place in His beautiful plan.

The Spirits of Nature dwell among each other to interact and bring all things together in peace and harmony. When we can walk or can live in the woodlands among the Nature Spirits, we begin to feel like we are a part of the mountain itself, joining our minds, bodies and Spirits with all the living things we find there.

God was the Creator of all the mountain splendor and left a part of Him in each living thing. In the end, being in a forest gives us the feeling of becoming one with God Himself.

Distant Memories

Once long ago, when the Earth was young,
I spoke a language of world-wide tongue.
I wore a toga and worked with a crystal,
And my homeland is now thought mythical.

Mu, Lemuria, Oz and Atlantis,
Were lands of a thriving metropolis.
Aircarts and spaceships were the traveling ways,
And even the unicorns sometimes would graze.

Next I remember as a Cherokee Brave,
As son of the Chief I had to behave.
Our tribe was diligent, peaceful and strong,
They still tell our tale in many a song.

Then I recall as a secret inventor,
I was known as the town's experimenter.
I worked all alone with the best of intentions,
And now people use many of my inventions.

Today, right now, I'm a child of light,
So I try to be good and do what's right.
I must live my life the best that I can,
Because that's the reason the Great Plan began.

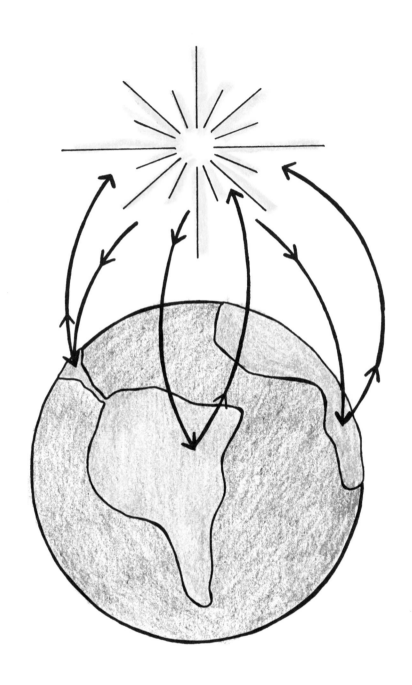

Message

The Wheel of Life is always turning. And the circles of rebirth are forever ongoing. After we left God's Spirit as the beautiful sparks of God, we came to Earth and entered human bodies. The God-Spirit living in these bodies can never, ever die; so when our physical body does die, our Spirit wishes to come again into another human form.

Our Spirits look all over the world and pick out a lady who is expecting a baby. When that baby is born, the Spirit gently lowers itself into the baby's body. Now the Spirit has a *second* physical life to live. This process of a Spirit being reborn again and again in different countries and of different races was planned by God. It is the only fair way our Spirits can learn important lessons from each different life and return as a better person each time.

In our final lifetime, we won't do any bad things to have to make up for and, when that last human form dies, our beautiful Spirit will finally be able to return to the Spirit of God and live in His Light forever.

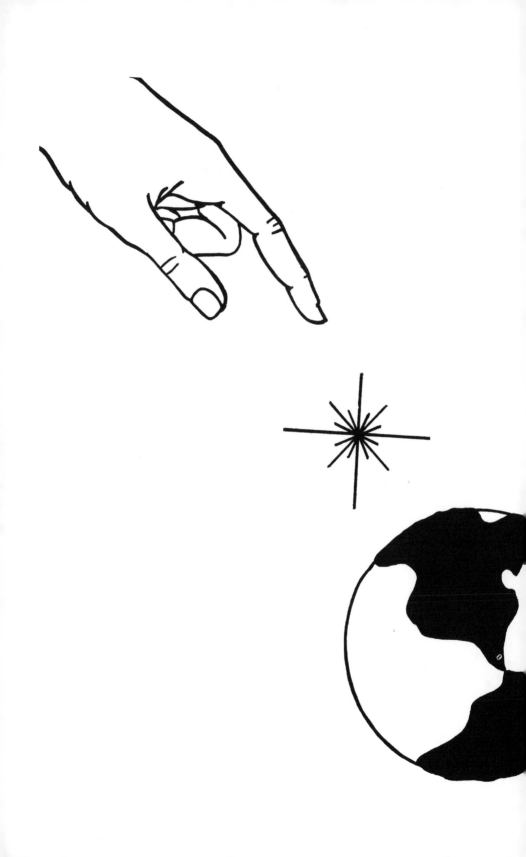

Guiding Lights

Comforter, Helper, Friend and Guide,
For every job he's most qualified.
He protects me from danger when I'm outside,
And from him my feelings I never can hide.

He's a Spirit of love all made up of light,
To help me in life to do what is right.
He was sent from God all glowing and white,
To stay around me like a satellite.

When I have a problem needing solutions,
He's always by me to give resolutions.
He shows me the way in my meditation,
For he's only here for my Spirit's salvation.

He's here to aid and be my helpmate,
And to my welfare he is dedicate.
In time of trouble he does not hesitate,
With God he helps me to communicate.

Thank you God for my loving Guide,
In whom I can trust, love and confide.
Thank you for my Guide so dignified,
Life is a comfort with him alongside.

Message

Ever since people have lived on the Earth, God looked after them in a very special way. To each and every person, God gave a Spirit to guide and watch over. Some people call these Spirit Guides by other names, like a Guardian Angel. It doesn't matter what we call them, the most important thing is that we know they are here to help us all.

It is God's will that we let the Guides do their work to help us in our lives. Their purpose is to work for God by guiding each person to live a good life. They also do much to protect and warn us when we are in danger.

If we are quiet and we still our minds and think of God, they will help us by guiding our Spirit through the right paths of meditation. Then our Spirit can soar up to God and, for just a moment, our Spirit and God's Spirit can touch each other.

Gifts Of The Trees

I'm a tree and I'm here for thee,
I cost no money, I charge no fee.
In this tale I tell about me,
So listen now, the knowledge is free.

As part of nature, God put me here,
All over the Earth I do appear.
I have many uses all through the year,
And my living gifts I volunteer.

From the sizzling sun, I give you my shade,
And in my arms, eggs of birds are laid.
My trunk holds burrows the squirrels have made,
And for shelter from storms, I kindly give aid.

My blossom's nectar the bees find sweet,
And my tender trunk, bears find a treat.
The morning sun my raised arms greet,
Now my use to man makes me complete.

My strong, straight wood is used for building,
And my juicy fruits are nourishing.
My many branches are used for warming,
And my seedlings are ever reforesting.

Next time you happen upon a forest,
Look around and feel greatly blest.
Whisper thanks to the trees as you rest,
Believe me, you'll make us the happiest!

156

Message

Trees, like so many other wonderful parts of Nature, are here for us to use and enjoy. God gave people countless natural things to make us happy. We must all learn to love and to be thankful for all of God's beautiful gifts.

We all take so many things for granted in this world that we also must take the time to look at the simple things like the trees.

Trees give us wood and, from that wood, we get so many wonderful things. From wood we make our houses and the furniture in those homes. We burn wood to keep our homes warm and snug in winter. From wood we make paper to write on, paper bags and cardboard boxes. Several of our tools have wood; rakes, brooms, shovels. The roots of the trees keep the soil together so we have wet and fertile ground to grow food. Different delicious fruits and nuts come from trees too.

You can see that just from one of God's natural gifts, we get shelter, food and warmth. Be kind to all of Nature, especially the bountiful trees.

Nobody Like Me

I could wear a white coat like a Doctor,
Or live in the grand house as a Governor.
I would be cheered by crowds as a Matador,
Or paint my face as a Warrior.
Of all the people in the world to be,
I'm glad I'm me 'cause I like me!

I could sail a ship as a Buccaneer,
Or glide a boat as a Gondolier.
I would scale the peaks as a Mountaineer,
Or wear plumed hats as a Musketeer.
Of all the people in the world to be,
I'm glad I'm me 'cause I like me!

I could live by the seas as a Fisherman,
Or fly with a cape like Superman.
I would cure the animals as a Veterinarian,
Or live in tall tepees as an Indian.
Of all the people in the world to be,
I'm glad I'm me 'cause I like me!

I could amaze the people as a Magician,
Or work with wires as an Electrician.
I would make big promises as a Politician,
Or play beautiful songs as a Musician.
Of all the people in the world to be,
I'm glad I'm me 'cause I like me!

I'm me and I can play calm or wild.
And my ways can be strong or mild.
My life and future are yet unstyled,
But best of all, I am God's child.
Of all the people in the world to be,
I'm glad I'm me 'cause GOD likes me!

Message

God dearly loves each and every one of His people. He loves the street cleaner just as much as the President of the United States or the Queen of England. We must always be proud of who we are and be kind and loving to all other people no matter who they are.

God made all five different races of people and He made all their skins a different color too. These skin tones are Red, Brown, Black, Yellow and White. God wanted to see just how well all his people would get along with each other.

We must never treat anyone badly because his skin color is not like our own. God loves all races of men equally and we must too. God also doesn't care what we do for a job either. A Janitor or Garbage Collector is just as good a job as a Lawyer or Doctor. What God looks at in a person is how kind and loving that person is. God looks to see how forgiving we are of each other too. We should not look on other people of the world as being Japanese, Africans, or Americans. We must only see each person as a beautiful shining part of God's sparkling Spirit.

Hey, I'm Alive!

Deep in a forest glen,
Around the lion's den,
Beside the dancing stream,
We're part of Nature's scheme.

I'm a plant, a flower, a weed,
And for our feelings we plead.
Just for *you* we thrive,
And say, "Hey, I'm alive!"

We can sense your feeling,
In vibrations you're sending.
We grow better when you're happy,
And it makes us feel so snappy.

Notice, feel and love us,
And over us make a fuss.
We love to hear you laugh,
Please do on our behalf.

We have feelings and moods,
So please do not be rude.
Just for *you* we thrive,
And say, "Hey, I'm *alive!*"

Message

All living things have energy. This energy sends out vibrations in the form of an aura. We know that plants and flowers are growing and living things. They have energy auras that can respond to our own aura vibrations.

If we are sad a lot, our plants will feel this sadness too. They won't grow well because of the sad vibrations they feel from us. We must always remember that all living things are a part of God's plan for people to live a happy life on Earth.

We should send good feelings and happy thoughts to all growing things. God loves us very much and wants all vibrations on the Earth to be good and happy ones. Just think how empty our land would look if all we had was bare dirt. Take the time out from your play to look at the beautiful flowers and plants and thank God for putting them here for you to smell, touch and admire.

The Importance Of Music

I can give you advice,
And ask for no price.
Maybe by chance,
I'll help you to dance.
I can help you be strong,
I am music and song.

If you're feeling unglued,
I will lift your mood.
If you're feeling low,
Your Spirit I'll glow.
I can help you be strong,
I am music and song.

I can make you feel pride,
And put bounce in your stride.
I can take away fears,
All through the years.
I can help you be strong,
I am music and song.

If you're inclined to weep,
I can put you to sleep.
If you feel in a laze,
My notes will daze.
I can help you be strong,
I am music and song.

If you want to give praise,
The Church we'll upraise.
Tenor or Bass,
Whatever the case,
I can help you be strong,
I am music and song.

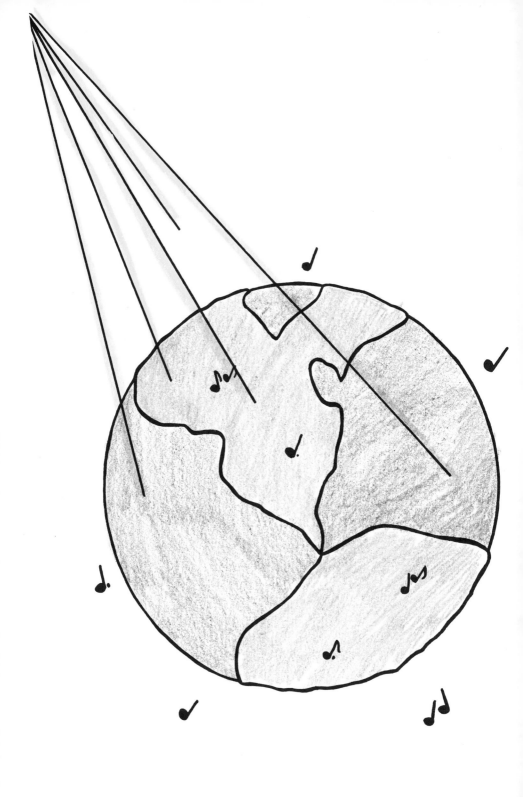

Message

God loves to hear music from His people. When we create any kind of harmonious music, we are sending out beautiful vibrations from our auras. When we sing, our auras look as good as we feel. Whenever you are sad or feel bad about something, listen to some happy music and soon you will be singing and feeling good again.

People who write songs and sing for a living are usually special people doing us all a very big favor. Some songwriters are very close to God and they write songs to tell us how we should live our lives in order to be closer to God's Spirit.

Music does many things. Music can comfort, soothe, excite and make us happy inside. People use music to put them to sleep and to wake them up. Without any note of music, the world surely would be a very dull, quiet and sad place to live.

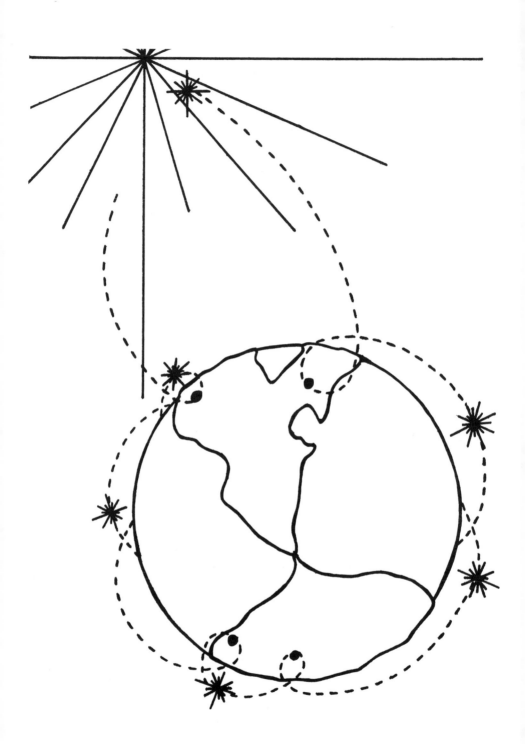

God's Plan

God wanted some company,
Then began Man's history.
God grew tired of the dark,
And our Spirits were His spark.

God wants us to return,
We have lessons to relearn.
We must not forget,
To repay every debt.

We must love all our brothers,
And be kind to one another.
We must respect all Nature,
'Cuz it came from the Creator.

Our way of life is clear,
To God's laws we must adhere.
This life we must endure,
To make our Spirits pure.

Once the circle has begun,
It turns and turns 'til God has won.
He will not set our planet's sun,
'Til all our Spirits with Him are one.

Message

In the very beginning, when our Spirits were sent out from God as sparks of His living Light, He always meant for us to one day return to Him and live forever in that beautiful Light. Our Spirits can only return to God if they are perfect and pure.

Each time we return to Earth for a new life, our Spirit has planned out just how we can be better so that we can get back to God faster. Since we do not always remember the plans that our Spirit made, we must live as good a life as we can. We must never miss a chance to help anyone. We must always treat everyone fairly and equally. If someone is mean to us, then we should pray for that person's Spirit. God said for us to love even our enemies and we must do that too.

It will be easier for us to love all people if we can just remember that God's Spirit is in each and every one of them. God has given us all a great strength. That strength is the Light of His Spirit living in us.

Part Four

Mother Nature's Babies

Mother Nature's Babies are all
the Nature Spirits who have special
duties to help Nature live and
interact in peace and harmony.

Part Four Contents

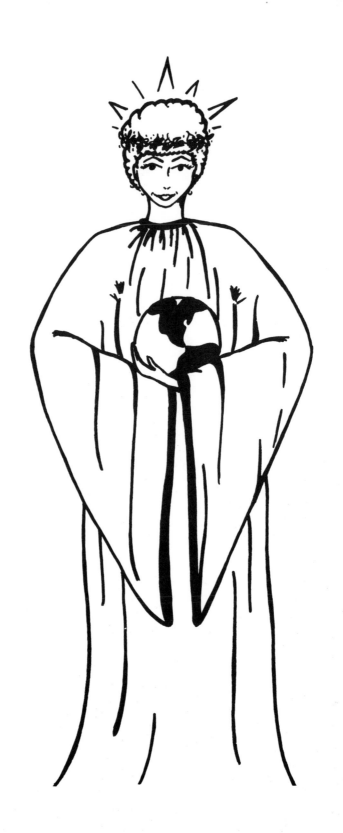

Mother Nature

Mothers are loving, kind and giving. Nature is the Earth and all forms of life living on it. Since the Earth is kind and giving to us, we call all the land and all the Seasons upon the land, Mother Nature.

Everywhere we look we see some signs of Mother Nature. She can be seen in the warming sun's rays, in the lazy drifting clouds, in the gently falling rains, in the cool green forests and in the grassy rolling hillsides.

Mother Nature is very alive in the deserts where the tall Saguaro cactus grows taller than a person and where desert flowers blossom and bloom their beautiful bright colors.

Thunderstorms, snowy nights, sunny days, moonlight shining on oceans, — all are faces of our Earth Mother that we call Mother Nature. Isn't she beautiful?

Mother Nature has so many, many different jobs to do, she hardly has time for them all. She had to have some very special helpers whom she calls her 'Babies.' She loves her babies very much and gave them a name. Mother Nature named them Nature Spirits.

Mother Nature, with the help of her Babies, paints the colors on the flowers each Spring. Every summer they help the bees gather their nectar. In the autumn, they arrange for the beautiful display of artwork on the tree leaves and bushes. And in winter, they cover all the lands with a glistening, white blanket of soft snow.

We must always be kind to our land and water to show our great appreciation to Mother Nature for all the love she has given to us.

Father Wind

Fathers are gentle, strong and comforting. The Wind is the part of Nature that moves over the whole Earth and is free in Spirit. Since the Wind can be gentle, strong and comforting, we call it Father Wind.

We can see signs of Father Wind almost everywhere we look. He can be seen shaking hands with the trees on an autumn afternoon. He can be felt by his gentle breath across our faces on a hot summer day. And his handicraft artwork can be seen and admired in his masterful carvings of the great Grand Canyon.

Father Wind often whispers and sings to us too. Have you ever heard his Wind Spirit whistle through rock formations? Have you listened to his whispers as he traveled through a forest of trees? The swishing of willows? The rustles of autumn leaves? Father Wind brings *sound* to Nature like no other Nature Spirit can.

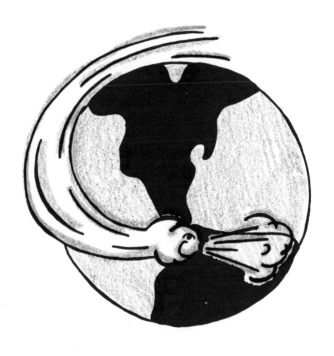

Father Wind is always so busy he never ever runs out of very important things to do. He has to travel all over the world to wherever he is needed. He works very hard all day and all through the night. He is as old as the Earth and always works harmoniously with Mother Nature to make our planet a wonderful place to live.

Father Wind gently lifts the seeds from the flowers and the trees to send them far and wide for Mother Nature to plant. He tugs at the autumn leaves and sends them scurrying and flurrying around the ground for the children to romp through. He blows softly on us to cool our heated faces in the summer sun. And in winter, he whirls and swirls the snow into sculptured drifts of sparkling splendor.

The Water Spirit

Have you ever wondered why being near water makes people calm? Have you ever wondered why you are so happy sitting beside a dancing stream? And why do people say a brook is babbling? Mother Nature knows why and she's going to tell you.

Long, long ago, the people of the land were very sad. Mother Nature saw this and it made her sad too. She decided to do something to cheer up all the saddened people. She sent a special Spirit to the Earth to live in all the waters of the land. She told this little Spirit to spread happiness and to make the hearts of all those who heard her glad inside.

Mother Nature gave this little happy Spirit a special name. She called it **Water Spirit**.

And so the little Water Spirit did as Mother Nature told her and she now lives within all the waters of the Earth. She lives in the great seas and comforts us when we hear the giant waves bounding up on the shores and thundering down over rocks.

She lives in each magnificent waterfall to gladden our hearts with the rapid splashings of her waters.

She lives in every stream winding through the lowland meadows and in the high mountain streams; babbling, chatting, sputtering and splashing; all the time spreading happiness and filling all our hearts with a peaceful joy.

Woodland Elves

Woodland Elves live in the forests and help all the little animals to be careful and stay happy. Mother Nature sent the Spirit Elves to Earth to help all her living creatures.

These little Elves are very small. They are so small they can stand in the palm of your hand. Mother Nature made them this tiny so that they can go anywhere they want to. Sometimes, they have to get into some very narrow places. The Woodland Elves are in charge of teaching, helping and caring for all the animals and little creatures of the land.

Just as all people have a Spirit Guide who watches over them, all animal creatures big and small, have a Woodland Elf to help them too. The Elves have so many, many jobs to do they're always very busy.

Springtime is their busiest season. They lead all the tiny honeybees to where the flower nectar is the sweetest. They help the baby fawns take their first steps. The silky white cocoons are carefully guarded by the Elves until the beautiful butterflies are free to flit about. And all the fluffy baby bunnies are kept from getting lost by the helpful Woodland Elves.

Flower Fairies

Once upon a time, when our Earth was very young, all living plants, flowers and trees were the same color -- a very dull grey. Mother Nature looked down and thought how beautiful the world would be if everything was a different color.

She called upon some of her Spirit Babies who liked to play with paints. These Spirits were always busy with thinking up new colors to paint with. Mother Nature named them *Flower Fairies*.

Since each Flower Fairy was in charge of a different color, Mother Nature said to them, "Go down on the Earth and spread your glorious colors on all living plants, flowers, trees and grasses. And when the seasons change, make the colors change too. Go and paint the morning and evening skies. Paint the deserts and the lonely mesas. Paint all you see. I leave the color decisions up to you."

And so the little Flower Fairies giggled with so much happiness. With painting pails and brushes in hand, they came to the Earth and spread all their wondrous colors all about. They had buckets and buckets of hues, tints and shades of every color.

The Fairies had such a fun time painting the tree trunks warm browns and chalky whites. Then they spread shades of lush green on each and every leaf. The flowers were gently brushed with tints of every soft color they had.

Just when they were all done, autumn had arrived. Now they started all over again with paints of orange, gold, red and yellow to dazzle the eyes of all who looked upon them.

Tree Nymphs

The dictionary tells us that a "nymph" is a "female Nature Spirit." A Tree Nymph is a girl Nature Spirit that lives among the trees. Mother Nature gave these special Babies of hers a very important task to do.

In the Springtime, when all the mother birds are busy building their nests, the Tree Nymphs gather twigs and pieces of straw to help the birds. And when the mother bird has to sit all day keeping her eggs warm, the Tree Nymphs bring her food.

After the eggs have hatched out and the baby birds are noisily chirping and peeping for food, the Tree Nymphs watch over the little baby birds while their mothers go out in search of food for them.

The most important job of all though, is when the baby birds decide they want to try to fly like their mamas. Their wings are not always strong enough to hold them up and sometimes the Tree Nymphs are ready to catch a falling fledgling and return it to its nest.

Mother Nature loves all the birds so she sent them the Tree Nymph Spirits to guard and watch over them.

Snow Pixies

Long ago, the season of Winter was very gloomy. All the lush trees were bare of leaves. The once green grass was brown and dry. And all winter long, everything was cold, grey and brown. "How drab everything looks!" said Mother Nature. So she decided then and there to dress winter up.

She called upon her Babies again. These she named *Snow Pixies*. These little Spirits were always very busy weaving beautiful designs out of a cold, white, fluffy material. Mother Nature went to them and said, "Do you think you could drop all your lovely designs on the Earth in winter? Your designs sparkle and glisten so, I'm sure they would make the dull winter turn into something beautiful!"

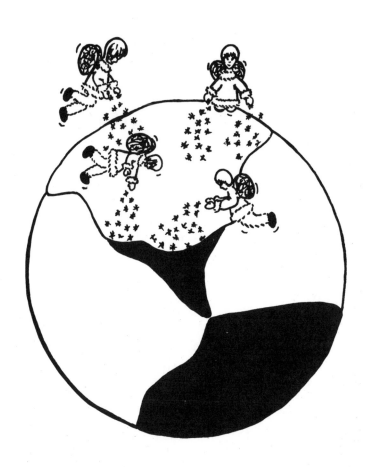

Well! I'll tell you! Those little Snow Pixie Spirits were just so excited! For now they had something to do with all those designs they were making. They busied themselves and made billions and billions of the snow designs and, when they were done, they sprinkled them from the clouds all over the dull, brown winterlands.

As it happened to turn out, the Snow Pixies had changed winter into a splendid world of glittering white. The snow made the whole land turn into a quiet, gentle hush. The snow became a natural blanket for many woodland creatures and it kept the bitter, blustering winds from their nests, burrows and dens. It also gave children whole new sledding, sliding and building games to have fun with. People figured out things to do with the snow too. They made up a ski game, made snowmobiles and snowshoes. Everyone was happy with all the Snow Pixie's work.

Nature Gnomes

Most people think gnomes are little, wee men who live underground and guard treasure. Actually, gnomes ARE little, wee men about as tall as your knee, but they surely don't guard treasure of silver and gold. Gnomes guard Mother Nature's treasure ... her animals.

Now, since these Nature Gnome Spirits are so small and are like little old men with long, silky beards; they can appear to look quite funny. Since Gnomes don't much like being laughed at, they take great care that people don't ever see them.

Mother Nature sent the Nature Gnomes to live on the Earth to care for all her beloved animals. She gave them a special home in her rich ground so that they could live all over and hear the cries of any creature that needed help.

It was the Nature Gnomes that put the white spots on the baby deer's back so that the little fawns would blend in with the forest floor to protect it from any enemies. The Nature Gnomes make noise in the woods to alert animals that hunters are nearby. They tell the animals to take cover and get into their homes when a storm is approaching. They are ever on the lookout for the scent of smoke and are the ones to alert the animals in the event of a forest fire. And they guard over hibernating creatures so that they can sleep through the long winter in peace.

If you SHOULD ever spy a Nature Gnome when you're deep in a woodland forest, please don't giggle at him. Tell him how much you appreciate all his loving work.

Rainbow Leprechauns

Many people in America will tell you that there is no such thing as a Leprechaun. You must go and ask the Gentle people of Ireland, for they truly DO believe in them. They even leave food out on their doorsteps at night for the Little People.

Mother Nature has found a very unique job for the little elf spirits called Leprechauns. They have taught the people on Earth the meaning of REAL treasure.

The tale was spread far and wide that the Leprechauns loved gold, and that they gathered and hid all this gold treasure in a big pot at the end of every rainbow.

Well, after many years of searching for the Leprechaun's pot of gold and never finding it, people lost all interest in it. Every time they got near the end of the rainbow, it would suddenly disappear.

The people now began to realize that the little Leprechauns were trying to teach them to appreciate the treasure of the magnificent rainbow itself. The people learned to love the gift of nature and not to look for selfish prizes that were never ever there at all.

The next time you see a beautiful rainbow in the sky, be thankful for all the good things you have in life. And don't forget to thank the little Leprechauns for the rainbow too!

Spring Sprites

A sprite is a small Spirit. The Spring Sprite was asked by Mother Nature to make sure that the Season of Spring each year went as planned.

We can thank the Spring Sprites for the sweetness they put into the first Spring day to tell us that the long days of winter are over with for another year.

They have an awful big job to do, for they not only prepare nature for the Season of Spring, they also help all the animals prepare too.

Have you ever wondered where the morning dew on the grass and flowers comes from? Well, it's all the doing of the Spring Sprites! Before the sun is awake, they sprinkle little drops of fresh water on all the newly-born flowers and grasses to give them drinks for the warm day ahead.

The Spring Sprites make sure every caterpillar is safe in its cocoon so the Woodland Elves can guard them until they become butterflies. They gently touch each and every tree bud so that the leaves can unfold to greet the sun.

They dance on the flower petals and every bloom sends out a different scent in return.

The next time you leave footprints over a blanket of fresh morning dew, whisper thanks to the Spring Sprite Spirits ... they'll always hear you.

Merry Mermaid

Mother Nature could see that all the creatures of the land were well cared for by her Nature Spirits. It gladdened her heart to see such a good job being done. "But what of all my sea creatures? Who will care for them?" said Mother Nature. "I will," said a lonely girl Spirit, "I would like to care for the little creatures of the Sea."

And so it was that Mother Nature gave the little Spirit girl a special body that would enable her to swim under all the seas and waters of the world. And Mother Nature named her *Mermaid*.

The little Mermaid was so happy to be able to help Mother Nature that she spent all her days spreading happiness among the creatures of the sea. She did a good job too!

Have you ever heard anyone talk about a "school of fish?" This means many fish of one kind swimming all together. We have the little Mermaid to thank for that because she taught them all to stay together for safety.

She taught the octopus to hide himself by squirting out black ink at his enemies. She showed the tiny tropical fish how to quickly dart in and out of the coral to escape from harm. She taught the big, grey porpoise to guide lost boaters to shore.

You will probably never, ever see this very merry Mermaid, because deep under the seas, she's having so much fun.

A Very Special Message

I would like to give all the children of the world who have such wonderful open minds and delightful beliefs a very special message.

Whenever you are deep in a woodland forest, be still and listen for the soft voices of nature all around you.

Let your tender Spirit dwell among the wonders you see before you.

Attune your ears to listen for the quietness and marvel at the new discoveries that your mind and Spirit will find there.

Never be frightened by any strangeness you may find, for all things were created for the gladness of your heart and beautiful Spirit.

If ever you SHOULD spy a painting Flower Fairy or a busy Tree Nymph Spirit, hold the memory of the sight in your heart as a special secret, for if you have seen such a one...you are indeed a very special child.

HAMPTON ROADS
PUBLISHING COMPANY, INC.

books that fascinate . . .

Would you like to be added to our mailing lists?
Would you like a copy of our catalog?
Would you like to be notified as we publish
new books by Mary Summer Rain?
Fill in this page
(or copy it, if you would prefer to leave this book uncut)
and mail to:

Hampton Roads Publishing Company, Inc.
891 Norfolk Square
Norfolk, VA 23502

[ ] Please send latest catalog

[ ] Please add me to the following mailing list(s):

    [ ] Books for the body

    [ ] Books for the mind

    [ ] Books for the spirit

    [ ] Books by _____

NAME _____

ADDRESS _____

CITY _____ STATE _____ ZIP _____